HAS ANYONE SEEN JACK?

by Tony Bradman

illustrated by

Margaret Chamberlain

FRANCES LINCOLN

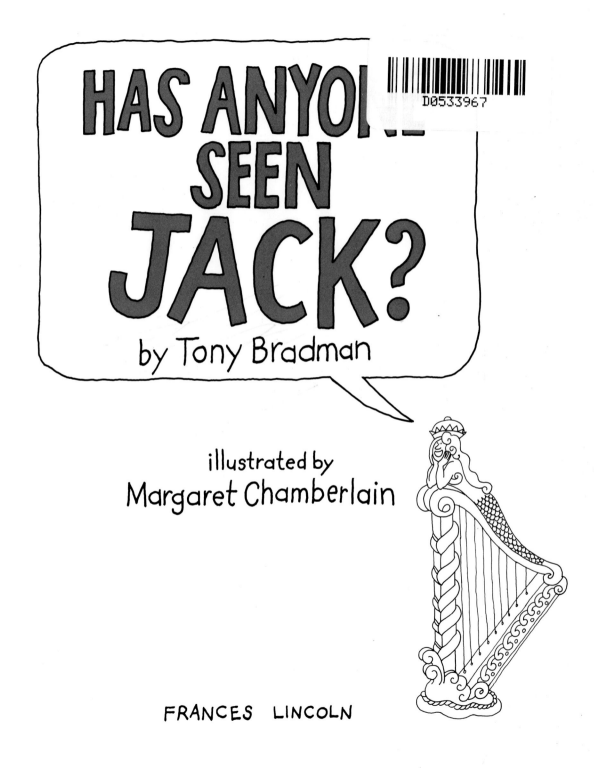

At the top of the beanstalk was the giant's castle.
Jack went inside...

MORE STORIES FROM
FRANCES LINCOLN CHILDREN'S BOOKS

THIS LITTLE BABY
Tony Bradman
Illustrated by Jenny Williams

'This little baby loves the morning, this little baby waves bye-bye…'
Parents and babies will have great fun together,
following these familiar moments from a baby's day.
A warm and appealing first picture book, based on a traditional rhyme.
ISBN 978-0-7112-2155-0

DON'T INTERRUPT!
Kathy Henderson
Illustrated by Sue Hellard

It's Saturday at home and Jim wants a drink,
but everyone is too busy to listen… "Don't interrupt!"
Lift the flap to see Jim's hilarious adventures
as he struggles on all by himself.
ISBN 978-0-7112-2154-3

These stories are available from all good bookshops.
You can also buy books and find out more about your favourite titles,
authors and illustrators on our website: www.franceslincoln.com